Barbara Byar moved to Ireland from America many years ago and now lives with her two sons and two dogs in County Kerry. An Irish Writers Centre Novel Fair winner, she's been listed for various awards, including: Over the Edge New Writer of the Year, the Bare Fiction Prize and the Ellipsis Zine Flash Collection competition.

Barbara has had short fiction published in numerous literary magazines and is a Guest Editor for VirtualZine, and a Senior Editor for BIFFY 50.

Founder and facilitator of the Thursday Night Writers group, Barbara has taught creative writing workshops for Kerry County Arts. She was also a participant in the inaugural X-Borders project.

Some Days Are Better Than Ours is her debut collection. She is currently working on her second novel.

SOME DAYS ARE BETTER THAN OURS

A Collection of Tragedies

Barbara Byar

Rock n Roll, Baby

rp

REFLEX PRESS

Barbara Byar

First published as a collection in 2019 by Reflex Press
Abingdon, Oxfordshire, OX14 3SY
www.reflex.press

Copyright © Barbara Byar 2019

A CIP catalogue record of this book is available
from the British Library.

ISBN: 978-1-9161115-3-0

1 3 5 7 9 10 8 6 4 2

Printed and bound in Great Britain by
Clays Ltd, Elcograf S.p.A.

Cover photographs by Ed Valfre
(www.edvalfresdreamland.com)

www.reflex.press/some-days-are-better-than-ours/

For Ronan and Liam

CONTENTS

Some Days Are Better Than Ours

Mummy lies on the kitchen floor, crosses her arms over herself and refuses to budge. Her baby belly rises like bread as her bum spreads over the spot where the lino has cracked and begun to peel. Maybe she wants to hide the hole. Maybe she will lie there till Dad fixes it. We don't know. She won't speak.

The cooker is on and open. Chicken nuggets and chips. Our favourite. Jimmy and I'd eat that every night if we could. On top of the white fridge, the kitchen timer click-clocks. Jimmy and I sit next to Mummy, cross-legged, one either side, and wait for the timer to go off.

Meanwhile, Dad's in the back garden, hammering away at something. Whether pounding nails, sawing wood or screaming, he's loud as Mummy's quiet. Same with Dog who barks and barks and barks. I peek out the window, head low so Dad can't see me. He's almost done boarding up the doghouse. A paw sneaks out from a small gap. Dad pelts it with the hammer and pounds up the final plank.

The timer buzzes and I slide the nuggets and chips onto plastic plates and put them on the glass table. Jimmy and I scramble up tall chairs, feet dangling, and eat with our fingers. I press the remote, and Marvin the Muffin comes on. Jimmy squeals and sings the theme song. He doesn't know many words yet, but he tries.

Dad stomps in, takes one look at Mummy, grunts, then goes straight out the front door. The car peels down the road. Maybe he'll come home. Maybe he won't.

On the telly, Marvin talks to two kids around Jimmy's age about their happiest day. One says, 'Every day when Mummy reads me a bedtime story.' The other goes on about the time his Dad took him to a soccer game.

Some days are better than ours.

Various Things That Crossed Her Mind

She would have been a physicist ballerina or even a ballerina physicist. If she could.

In her dreams she pirouettes through galaxies, leaps through dimensions, lands with a thump on a wooden stage in a parallel universe. Bows.

Geometry is the hardest math: all sharp Picasso angles and infinite Spirograph loops cut with linear equations. Like the string art her father made in the '60s with nails and neon thread mounted on painted plywood. They still hang on the basement walls. She doesn't understand any of it, and whatever they say about ninety-year-olds getting their college degree, it's probably too late at fifty. She should have just joined the Army like her father said. At least then she'd know how to fire a gun.

Radon is the heaviest gas. Rampant as bog turf in the Southwest of Ireland. You can't see or smell it, but it seeps into your foundation, insidious like the voice in your head which says it's not just a cough, it's cancer.

Matisse reminds her of L.A. She likes neither. Mostly because she needs sunglasses for both. Sunglasses and a silk scarf wrapped round her head like Tippi Hedren in *The Birds*, but that took place at the other end of California up in Bodega Bay. She'd been there once. Driven up the coast with her ex who now calls himself Wolfgang. Hitchcock was the modern apocalypse auteur, but no one did it as good as Bosch.

Bosch is also a German white goods manufacturer. There may be a connection. She never uses her dishwasher anymore now that everyone's gone.

Don't forget to give the postie and binmen a card for Christmas. Slip a tenner in; it's the least you can do. Everyone loved that one postie who looked like Christian Bale but got hit in the head playing rugby and fell dead a few months later. Aneurysm – supposed to be a good way to go. Poe's 'The Cask of Amontillado', the worst.

Chocolate will never be sweet as revenge.

No matter how much they love you, dogs will eat you if they must.

Sex only becomes good once it's no longer something done to you. Unless you are the one who is doing. Love is a need not a solution, and if she could do it all again, she would cross that sticky dive-bar floor, kneel before his wheelchair and say, 'Come on, let's go.'

At night, she dances before the mirror and cries to the universe, 'Help me. I am alone.'

Everything dies. Nobody really cares.

Dreams are the only reason we wake.

Porcelain

War has not come to this city, but like the twisted path of the abortionist's wire, the scars are there. It has taken their men and replaced them with strangers: refugees from levelled cities; prisoners of war. Once 600,000 strong, the city has swollen to twice that number.

None is her Frederick.

There are so many. Why should she care for them? Give them food? They huddle in abandoned factories and railway stations. How do they deserve a roof when their men – no, her man: Frederick, darling Frederick, so handsome and tall, too young to die – freeze on the Russian front?

Hannah's boots are flat so she won't trip on the cobblestones as she works her way towards Friedrichstadt, the factory district where the American POWs are kept. She prefers feeding the POWs, though they deserve it less. The refugee shelters are full of children screaming for their missing mothers. At least the POWs are silent.

They are lucky to have porridge. Where has it come from? The railways are broken, contorted by bombs. The city has no farms, only palaces, museums and towering cathedrals. Florence on the Elbe, or so they say. Hannah would not know; she has never been to Italy.

She sees no faces, only bowls: dented, cracked, leaking; held forward for her ladle by trembling hands, thick with crusted dirt. The bowls clang against each other as they shake for her attention. Hannah goes as fast as she can, not daring to look in their eyes.

There are no individuals in war, only multitudes; an endless sea of need and futility. So many, all similar in their differences: the colour of their skin; their accents; the stench. Until one hand catches her eye: a clean hand, white as porcelain, the veins threading the skin like the intricate designs of the city's famed china. Hannah looks up then.

His blonde hair, so pale, his eyes a thousand shades of blue. 'Frederick?'

Hope is the luxury of possibility. Hannah meets his urgent gaze and sees what she wants to see. He smiles the same crooked smile as Frederick, and she is lost.

The sirens scream for the 160th time. Hannah jerks, nearly drops the bucket. 'Don't be afraid,' he says in English, but she hears German. His warm breath puffs tiny ghosts into the cold air. When his long, white fingers brush her arm, his touch is like ice, like her frozen husband.

For the 160th time, no bombs fall.

The next morning, Hannah sips her steaming tea. She trails a finger along the rim of the cup. It seems a lifetime ago that she had worked at the factory. In the cold of her room, it was difficult to remember the radiant heat of the kilns as they burned at fourteen hundred degrees. She misses the warmth.

It is easier than she thought to smuggle him from the camp. Easier still to keep him in her empty, attic apartment. His name is Mark, but he does not mind that she calls him Frederick. Hannah is smart enough to know he doesn't love her and wise enough not to care. When the sirens sound, she no longer wonders if the warning is real.

A few weeks later, it is Fasching, Germany's Mardi Gras. The city bustles with excitement. In their fancy dress, it is easy for the women to pretend there is no war. Even the refugee children shriek with joy as they run down the streets, trailing colourful streamers, stopping only to dip their fingers in buckets of sugar, saved for the occasion.

Hannah removes her costume from the trunk and dresses in the room once meant for the babies she never had. Not yet. Maybe not ever. She piles her long, blonde hair on top of her head, fishes makeup from the bottom of a drawer, and steps into the dress.

Mark stands naked in the sitting room, drying his hair with a towel. He gasps when Hannah emerges but does not move. She must go to him. She touches his face with soft hands and trembles when he kisses her.

They don't hear the sirens at first and ignore them when they do. As a pilot, he is the first to hear the planes.

'Come, Hannah.' He grabs her hand and leads her to the door.

They are naked, but he does not let her dress, only grabs a blanket to wrap around her. The stairwell is empty as they scramble down; the neighbours on the street, enjoying Fasching. He takes her to the basement where it is cold and damp.

'We will be safe here,' he says and draws her close.

When the bombs drop, the roar is like the marching armies of hell. White light flashes at the small windows, and he tightens his grip around her. The screams of the revellers morph from glee to terror to silence. Concrete crumbles as the building above is hit. Dust fills the air, and it is difficult to breathe. It is hot, too hot; she is suffocating. Sweat dripping down her face, she shrugs off both him and the blanket.

'Hannah.' His pale, white hand crawls through the dust towards her as Hannah feels her innards bake.

'Mark,' she pants, acknowledging him for the first and last time, her voice burnt porcelain in a roaring kiln.

I Eat the Flowers on Your Grave

My baby's breath rose from the cold, hard ground, steaming like that carriage horse in Central Park. The one I didn't want to ride.

'It's cruel. Did you never read *Black Beauty*?'

'It's my birthday. Would you deny me, Lily? This one birthday?' His last birthday. We knew it then; remember it now.

His two lips nestled my neck like the bit in the horse's jaw. 'I could kiss you forever on a night like this. Forever and ever and ever.' Snorting snap as the reins jerked back; mist blurring the streetlamp lightning flash – 'Oh, Lily. It hurts. It hurts so bad.'

Cold blew through me, a wind on ice-sheathed bracken, and I clasped his hands under the wool blanket which stank of horse and resignation. 'We'll go skating tomorrow at Rockefeller Centre.' All the way from Ireland for this last dream. 'I'll carry you if I must; you're light enough.'

He nodded, head bobbing, bit unbitten, two lips a rictus of pain.

On the hospital bed, heart clap clop clopping like hooves through the cold, dark night – 'There'll be no Christ anthems at my funeral, Lily. No fucking flowers. No song and dance. Don't let my mother at it. Thirty years since I believed those fairy stories. Stick me in an oven; maybe then I'll be warm. Climb to the barracks top of Bolus Head and let me fly, fly across the ocean like all our dreams unbroken.'

Our kid curled like a beat dog in the daffodil-yellow chair. 'They think yellow's gonna cheer me?' He's powerless to reach him, to touch that gentle, slumbering head one last time. Light low in deep hours, his last, fierce entreatment – 'Please, God. Please, God, save me. I don't wanna die.'

Black beauty hearse horse snorts by the gravestone. His mother beseeches, trying to take me from him one last time. 'Jesus, Lily, come away with you now. Father, do something.'

My baby's breath – the ground fog, dew cold and crackling in icy filigree. Rose thorns rip my throat as I swallow, like the tangled clutch of the thing that killed you.

All the Things We Cannot Say

Tommy had known Lissy for as long as he could remember (and he remembers *everything*) but had never been able to look her in the eye. Not even now as she stroked his cold hand. All he could do was tremble and stare at the ground where they'd tossed his clothes and smashed all those bottles.

Lissy smelled of pizza and cake and summer – all Tommy's favourite things. All strong smells. Happy. They almost masked the smell of pee and poo running down his legs.

Lissy's breath was warm on his face. The face that wouldn't look up. Couldn't. Lissy sniffed like a dog and oh, no, her smell changed. Now, it was dead roses mulched in fresh dirt. Now, it was just like them after they'd tied him up.

They'd laughed. Tommy had laughed too. After all, it was just a game. But that smell...

'Oh, Jesus. Jesus. Jesus,' Lissy was trying to undo the ropes. 'Tommy, I can't get them loose, they're all wet and swollen.' Lissy sniffed her fingers and retched like Mum when she cleaned his bed.

Was she crying? He didn't want to make her cry.

'Stay here. I'll go get help.'

A frog croaked from Tommy's throat, and he began to shake as much as the ropes would let him. The rough fibres sandpapered flakes of his bare skin which drifted in the fading light like whittled wood.

'It's okay.' Lissy's hand was puppy-fur soft on his bare arm. He loved his puppy. Her name was Lissy.

Lissy took her coat off and draped it over him the best she could. It slipped to the ground soon as she left. Tommy tried not to be scared. Tried not to remember their faces like Halloween masks and mean words like the late-night programmes Mum and Dad watched.

'Don't go, Lissy,' Tommy said, so quietly he thought he was dreaming. Tommy loved his dreams which were almost always of Lissy, but the dusk between the time he closed his eyes and his dreams came – that was scary. It was dusk now. Dusk with his eyes open.

Tommy leaned back against the tree; drew comfort from the rough wood against his skin. It would all be worth it when Lissy saw what he had done. It had taken him days and three kitchen knives, but it was everything he could never say.

Tommy smelled Lissy before he saw her, an excited curry and cola smell. Tommy was excited too. He forgot about his skin raw under ropes, soggy underpants drooping, the cold.

'Fucking retard.'

That voice. It was Martin. Martin who collected Lissy in his LOUD Chevy Camaro with the V8 engine and 435 horsepower that smelled of grease. Martin who had tied him up.

20

'You can't say that.' Lissy sounded angry. Angry like his mum had been when she found the broken knives.

Martin came into view first, and their eyes met before Tommy could look away. *Don't you say a word,* Martin's eyes warned, *or I will kill you.* Tommy looked at the hunting knife in Martin's hands and kept his mouth shut.

Martin sawed through the rope, and Tommy was soon free. He didn't rub his sore arms or reach for his clothes. He had to be brave. In the dying light, Tommy pretended the dusk was dimming and he was dreaming, then looked up and into Lissy's face as she saw the carving in the wood his body had hidden. The delicate heart with their names enclosed:

Tommy loves Lissy

First Lissy looked at Martin, and her smell was a skunk hit by a car. Then slowly she turned to Tommy, and he, shivering and cold, was brave and did not look away. Full of tears, Lissy's eyes were sky just after night. And her smell? Her smell was of all the things she could not say and all his dreams come true.

I Walked 10,000 Worlds for You

A True Story

The first time she noticed? Rachel couldn't remember. A week ago, or ten. There, at the bottom of her short drive, a lone cigarette butt, filter baby-puke yellow. It was in an odd spot on a sliver of grass where fence post met path. She'd tossed it in the bin and forgot about it until the next morning when there was another in the same spot.

Just the one.

It wasn't until the fourth or fifth time that she began to take any notice. None of the neighbours on their small council cul-de-sac owned up to it though most smoked. Rachel stopped picking them up to see if they'd accumulate, but there was only ever the one.

Ever.

*

I have searched for you forever. Walked 10,000 worlds to find you. Swam Saturn's seven seas; crawled the nine circles of Hell, until there you were – in a small garden at the bottom of a blue hill, sun haloing your hair like the Alenethean wave crests in the ninth temporal zone.

I am forest fires raging; Ecuadorian roses blooming; lost love rejoining. I am here. Close your eyes.

Smell me.

*

When was the last time it had snowed? Rachel couldn't remember. Flurries swished every winter but rarely stuck. So she was surprised by three things that December morning: startling awake at 4 a.m.; pulling back the lined curtains to a world aglow from full moon on fresh snow; and a set of footprints directly under her window.

Under normal circumstances, Rachel would have been terrified, but she was under the spell of a melancholy moon and that strange waystation between dream and consciousness. The next thing she knew, she was out the front door examining the lonely footprints which led to her window then away again.

Rachel drew her house robe tight and followed the prints straight to the top of the estate and down the road to a small park where they ended in a copse of evergreens. The air was calm as the last stroke of midnight, but still the branches rustled. Not much. Only as if a tiny bird had landed.

Fresh snow began to fall, drifting like memories through insomnia. She opened her mouth and put out her tongue. Tasted ashes.

*

King of many Kingdoms, you are my only treasure. Anything. Everything, to kiss the snowflake tears from your lashes; protect you from cold's cruelty.

I am salty tears stinging; broken kisses burning; sympathy soothing. I am here. Close your eyes.

Taste me.

*

Rachel woke to the twins giggling. She threw open her bedroom window to give out to them only to find they'd built a snowman and dressed it in Richard's old clothes.

'Look, Mom,' they said, cheeks ruddy, eyes gleaming, 'it's Daddy.'

Rachel smiled and closed the window. She shook off her strange dream and shrugged on her house robe. How had it gotten wet?

Downstairs she put porridge on for the twins. As she stirred in honey, something soft but deliberate brushed against her ankle. Startled, she looked down, but there was nothing.

Time to lay traps again.

*

Many moons I've known you; through lightyears unforgotten. Melancholy bathes on your shores; let me swim in your beauty, sigh from your pores.

I am hearth fire crackling; desert sands baking; sunlight streaming. I am here. Close your eyes.

Feel me.

*

It was the twins' last day of primary school, and Rachel was trying to make the most of the quiet before the relentless roar of the summer holidays. At the kitchen table, she was drawing in charcoal from an old photo of Richard when something exploded.

Heart racing, eyes darting, she found the remnants of Richard's heavy-crystal ashtray scattered on the sideboard, the pieces still humming.

'Richard?'

*

I have knocked upon your every door. Cried a century or more. For all this and more, I can only implore.

I am lonely gales howling; forest leaves falling; moonlit surf crashing. I am here. Close your eyes.

Hear me.

*

All Hallows' Eve and embers still glowed in the fireplace when Rachel woke on the sofa. She put the metal fireguard in front of the fire and went up to bed. It was freezing in the bedroom, and her breath came out in foggy mist despite the thermostat reading twenty degrees. She checked on the twins, but they were toasty and warm in their room.

Rachel pulled a linen box from under the bed, blew away the slight film of dust, and opened it to the smell of lavender paper and her perfume. She pulled out her honeymoon negligee, slipped it on and lay on the bed, uncovered. Closed her eyes...

*

'Rachel, I am here. See me.'

*

And in her dream, they open.

Sex Life – Part One

Come here. I wanna show you something. Relax. Don't worry.
I'm not gonna hurt you.

*

What do you call it? That tingling? When the babysitter makes
you shower. Towels you dry. Rubbing. Rubbing. Robbing. You
are five, maybe six, when he lays you down on the bed to play
doctor. Finger in mouth, your four-year-old brother watches.
What does he remember? You remember everything. Over
and over and over. Do you like it? Maybe. Do you know
enough not to?

Your eyes close, your mind goes.

There.

The kids in the bushes rubbing. The brother and sister in
their basement touching. That girl who lay upon you,
humping.

Passed around. Around. Around. Around. Around. Around
like a merry-go-round.

*

Wanna massage?

What's that?

It's nice. I give them to your mother. She said it was okay.

You take in his hippie hair, dirty, dangling with beads, the scent of something (now known as patchouli, how you hate it hate it hate it). He leads you to the massage table (bed), lays you down. The sucker pucker of the oil bottle as it squirts. The sloppy slurp on your skin. Rubbing. Rubbing. Robbing. Arms, legs. Higher. Higher. His fingers fumble like spiders spinning. Probing.

Have you had your period yet?

What's that?

Nevermind. Your turn now. Hold out your hand.

Warm oil on your cold hand. Burning.

Go on. Touch it. Rub it. That's it.

Up. Down. Around. Around. Around.

There's one last place I haven't massaged. It's the best place.

Lie down.

*

You're a guest at the private pool on the swank estate. You're allowed to swim but only if the lifeguard inspects you. Makes sure you're clean. Clean enough to make you dirty.

Jump.

Clean yourself in the deep end. Sink.

Down.

Down.

Down.

Drown.

All fours next to the armchair for your back rub. Family scattered like cushions in the room. When no one's looking, Grandfather reaches down. Around. Rubbing. Robbing. It feels good. That's why you keep going back. You should know it's wrong. His hand shoots up anytime someone looks, comes in the room. Speaks.

His breath smells of butterscotch.

He corners you in the hallway. The bathroom. Takes you for drives to the lake. He has a hole cut in his pocket for your hand.

Up. Down.

Around.

Eyes closed. Mind goes.

Anywhere, please.

But there.

Nails

When did he start? Seven, maybe eight?

All Ben remembered was standing in the kitchen doorway – blood pooling metallic at the base of his gums, pulpy front tooth, loose for a week, now a guaranteed Tooth Fairy dollar in his extended palm – when Henry's fist whiplash cracked his mother's head into the kitchen table.

'I fucking told you...' Henry screamed, but all Ben heard was Mum's whimpers. All he saw was the blood tear-dropping down her white shirt as she pried her tooth from the wood with her fingernails.

Yeah. That was it. That's when he started biting his nails. By the time he was ten, he'd eaten them clean away and started on his toes.

'Jesus fucking Christ! The freak! The bloody freak.' Henry ranted downstairs as Mum tucked him into bed.

Moonlight streaming through broken-blinded window much as tears through her makeup, Mum tried to take his hands, but Ben stashed them between his legs.

'Why, son?'

Ben shrugged. 'Why'd you marry Henry?'

'I didn't want you to grow up without a Dad.'

'I don't want a Dad.'

By thirteen his toenails were gone too. He was gnawing calloused skin when he heard Mum in the back garden.

'How will he learn if you don't teach him? Please, Henry?'

'Useless cunt. The only thing he knows how to do right is fuck everything up. Now piss off and make me a cuppa.' Palm branded red on Mum's face, Henry returned to putting up his new motorbike shed.

Ben was waiting when Mum brought Henry his tea.

'I've no more nails left, Mum,' he said, still pressing the empty nail gun into the back of Henry's bloody head.

The Heart of Darkness

There is a silence in snow, and once the screaming stopped, she could hear it. Under thump pump of pounding heart and dense fog of panting breath.

Silence.

Behind her, the station lights flickered and fizzled like a poltergeist on crack. Ahead, perpetual night brewed thicker than the silence. August, the height of winter, the heart of darkness.

Run, Cali. Run.

They called her Cali 'cause she was from California; somewhere she never had to worry about freezing to death. Why had she ever left? Come to this godforsaken place? Hell is not hot; it's a desert of ice bathed in darkness. Hell was whatever the fuck was in the station.

Cali ran, cold squeezing with every laboured breath. She had one last chance to escape. One.

She made it to the CAT, scrambled into the tractor's cab, then stared at the key in her hand. So much for that plan –

she'd no idea how to drive one of these beasts. They had people for that. Had.

Figure it out. How hard can it be?

Her hands began to tremble; adrenaline generated heat for only so long. Tentacles of ice clutched and constricted, and she steam-engine puffed as her fingers flapped around the dashboard searching for the ignition. Breath crystals frosted the windows like an Antarctic coffin. She wouldn't last long.

Give up.

'No.' Resistance ghosted from her just as the cab door smashed open and Susan blew in, dragging the door closed behind her; in one hand a flashlight, the other a gun.

Too late. Too late. Oh, God. Too late.

'Cali? Jesus. Gear up quick. There's spare behind the seat.'

'Susan?' Cali couldn't stop shaking. 'Oh, God, Susan? I thought everyone was dead.'

'No time. You have the key?' Susan's eyes were frantic as they darted between rear window and Cali. 'Cali, move!' Susan snatched the key from Cali's trembling hand and tried to scramble past her in the cramped cab.

'Get some fucking gear on.' Susan started the engine, blasting light and cold air into the cab.

Cali fumbled behind the seat, struggling to grasp anything with her bone-numb fingers while Susan slap-dashed the control panel. The gears.

'Come on, you fucker.' Susan pulled an ice scraper from somewhere and went maniacally at the frosted glass. 'Goddamn blowtorch is what I need.'

Thank God, she didn't scrape the back window. If anything followed, Cali didn't want to know. She locked the door so there'd be no more surprises. Feeling had begun to return to her now gloved hands, and they hurt.

'Where will we go?' Cali said. Up to that point, she hadn't thought further than AWAY.

'Fucking anywhere but here.' Susan had cleared the screen enough to expose the darkness beyond.

Cali pointed through the window. 'What's the point? We'll never find our way out of here.'

'Red and blue flags mark the traverse to McMurdo Station,' Susan flipped switches with a flourish, and headlights cleared the darkness for about ten feet. But it encroached; someone, *something* was lurking. Waiting. Like the gun unspoken between them on the seat.

Grab it.

'And if we can't see them, we've got the GPS. Don't worry. We're out of this fucking fucktard hellhole. NOW!' Susan put the CAT into gear, and they crunched forward. The noise was incredible, but anything was better than the silence. Cali tensed. Waited. There was no way the thing wouldn't hear them. How would they ever escape unnoticed?

'Isn't Vostok closer?'

'Vostok? Are you kidding? I'd say that's where it came from. Fucking Russians never should have drilled into that lake.' Susan turned on the GPS and set their course. 'McMurdo is our best bet.'

But McMurdo was at least thirty days away even without dragging a trailer.

'Gas?'

Susan grunted. 'I sent a distress signal. They'll meet us halfway.'

The motor chunka chugged as the wind picked up, its howling a thwarted beast. Susan punched the dash. 'Oh Christ, a fucking storm.'

Cali wasn't afraid. She wasn't even cold anymore. Halfway into the parka, her eyes were lead. If she were home, she'd be at the beach soaking up the sun. God, the sun. Anything to see it once more. Cali closed her eyes and was back in Santa Monica, sun beating down, sand warm between her toes, dozing to the sounds of the surf and children laughing. She was so warm. So tired.

Come get me, motherfucker, just let me sleep.

'Cali? Cali! Don't sleep. Don't you fucking sleep!'

*

Cali opened her eyes to silence. They were no longer moving. The stop must have been recent because the windscreen had not yet frosted. The storm had passed, and the sky was clear. Stars diamond-glittered and aurora flashed razzle-dazzle like runway flags across the heavens. So beautiful after an eternity of darkness. Slowly, breath filigreed ice across the glass until they were once again entombed. The air was still, the clattering wind and pelting ice, silent.

One heart beat in the darkness, and it was not her own.

Bear

Bear was my friend, best and only. With me always. Soft fur satin against my wet cheek, I told her all my secrets. The rest, she saw. Bear didn't judge. She knew there was nothing I could do. Knowing that, I could let it be done.

Bear couldn't talk, her mouth was sewn shut, but her never-closing, black button-eyes assured me everything would be alright. That's where I looked. Each time. Every time. In Bear's eyes. In Bear's eyes, I was a jewellery box princess, spinning; the angel atop the Christmas tree, glowing; a mermaid flicking her tail, glimmering.

Sometimes, after, when I cried in Bear's arms, snot snarling her fur, I'd hear Bear in my head. Was I mistaken? Hearing things? Imagining? Her voice was deep and growly like a bear. Not scary though. Never. Not to me.

If I had claws, Bear said, *I'd scratch his face off.* But Bear had no claws, only soft pads of velvet and those could do nothing but stroke. Stroke the sticky puddles and pain away.

If I had teeth, Bear said, *I'd bite that thing off and swallow it whole.* But Bear had no teeth, only red thread for lips and pink felt for a tongue.

How could you not hear? Why were you not afraid? Why did you smile? Didn't you know Bear wanted to rip you to pieces?

Each time now. Every time. Bear growled and roared in frustration. It hurt my head and heart. So, I helped her. I had to. I was scared at first. I didn't want to hurt Bear, but she told me what to do. Assured me everything would be alright. So, I did it. Snuck scissors, needle, thread. Knives. Made Bear some claws. Some teeth.

And Bear was good as her words in my head. She clawed his face. Tore that thing off and ate it.

I miss Bear. Miss her a lot. But they wouldn't let me bring her. Said she was evidence. What's that? She's not evidence. She's Bear. My friend, best and only.

Opium

She wore a black dress and Opium. Nothing else. Not even shoes as she tottered along the edge of the balcony, empty bottle dangling from vodka-floppy fingers. Music like champagne bubbles drifted from the loft.

'What's the view like, Em?' he said from a silver chair, legs stretched before him, tuxedo lapels shining in the moonlight like bat wings.

'The stars are bigger. Closer. I almost feel I could touch them...' She stretched. Strained against the metal railing which dug into her thigh. The vodka bottle slipped from her fingers. It seemed forever before they heard the crash.

'Hope that wasn't my car, Em. I've grown quite fond of it.'

She giggled. 'You've had it for a week.'

'Longer than most things,' he said and lit a cigarette, his smoke rings expanding like moon halos around her swaying figure.

'Do you love me, Ian?'

'Always and forever,' he said, watching her legs. It was somewhere between late and early, and mist had begun to collect on the guardrail. He'd had just enough scotch to be unalarmed but not enough to forget she was there.

'I will be a star someday, won't I, Ian? I'll shine so bright, so hard, so long.' She stretched one arm and leg like a ballerina.

'Muffin, you're already a star,' he said and yawned. There was nothing tragic about her. No haunted past, no rapey cousin, not even a dead dog. She was just a pretty thing, shining brightly like all the other stars in the sky.

'Look, Ian,' she said, smack haze lifting from her voice, 'a shooting star.'

'Catch it,' he told her. 'Make a wish. All your dreams will come true.'

She laughed, then leapt. 'I got it, Ian,' she said as she fell with a flutter. Not like a sparrow but a crow. Swallowed by the mist, it was forever before he heard the crash.

Hope that wasn't my car, he thought and lit another cigarette.

Resurrection

You're in the coffin, powdered skin on white satin. A rouged grin can't clown your rictus frown.

'I hate you, you little piece of shit. Wish you'd never been born. If abortion had been legal, you would have been scraped from your mother's shrivelled womb and burned. I tried to convince her to get rid of you. Knew a fella who would do the deed for twenty bucks and a bottle of Jacks, but she refused. Gave her a good knock or two in the belly, but you were a tenacious fuck.'

Skin puddles on your finger bones. Would they crack and crumble if you hit me now?

'Take a swing at me, will ya? I'll fucking murder you, you useless cunt. Come here now, look what you made me do. A damn hole in the wall. Your ma will go mad, so she will, but I tell you what. I'm gonna leave it there. Leave it there to remind ya.'

Veins bled white. No blood left to splatter. No skin bruising night. No terror under the sheets listening for that heavy footstep on the creaky stair.

'What the fuck's this? A book? A fucking book? At least be a man and read a porno or something. What do you need a book for? You're

thicker than a bag of rocks. Sixteen now. Get a fucking job, you freeloader. Join the Army. I'm signing you up in the morning. Read fucking books on my back. Over my dead body.'

They close the lid. I watch you burn. Go home. Put the urn on the table. It's plain. Black and silver like your watch on my wrist.

'What's this?' she says.

'What the fuck do you think it is? Do you not know where I was, you stupid bitch?'

I give her an old backhand, but the cunning cow moves, and I hit the urn instead. It flies. Whacks the small one in the head, covers him in dust.

'Whatcha crying for, you little sissy. Grow a pair for fuck's sake and quit your whining before I stick you out in the shed again.'

That shuts him up quick alright, but I slap him all the same, just for the look in his eyes.

Touch

'So that's it, then?' Her eyes followed the dozens of hairline cracks running through the ceiling. When they'd moved into the new house, the plaster had been smooth as her forehead. Now both displayed the wear and tear from five years of settling.

He lay next to her on the bed, leg strewn over her side of the cast-off duvet, boxers a bunch under his balls, and searched her profile for an inkling of surprise or consternation, any emotion at all.

Nothing.

'There's no one else,' he said, face so close her blonde hair stirred with his every breath. He longed to reach out and stroke it as he had done a thousand times before. If only she turned to him. If only she stretched the long fingers of her hand one centimetre, so they connected with his thigh. If only she cared that he was leaving her forever.

'There never is,' she said and got up to dress for work.

'Alex?' he said. It was his day off. He had many of those. Plenty of time to think. To wonder. To yearn for purposeful touch of her skin.

She turned to him then, but her eyes were glass. 'Just push the key through the mail slot,' she said and went downstairs. Suddenly cold, he wrapped the duvet around himself.

*

Alex made herself a coffee, stirring the spoon a few times more than necessary. A bit splashed on the crease between thumb and forefinger. She stuck it in her mouth and sucked on it. Picked up the coffee, then put it down again, untouched. The door closed gently behind her when she left.

*

He spent most of the day walking around the city, each street mustering memory. Everywhere, her ghost, like a dream upon waking. In the early days, they'd danced in every club, eaten in every restaurant, fucked in every park. Somewhere along the way, somewhere in the thick bushes, expensive meals and throbbing nightclubs he'd lost her.

He was leaving, but she was the one who had gone.

*

Alex rarely left the office for lunch. Today she wasn't hungry, but when one o'clock rolled around, she had to get out.

She wandered, something she hadn't done in months, years even. These days every movement, every thought served a purpose. She had such little time left. Why didn't he see? She was hardly going to tell him. Once they had been so close, they'd read each other's minds, a touch of the hand the only necessary confirmation.

Instead of reaching out, he was leaving. Fine. So be it.

She ended up on a bench in the city park. A wide boulevard, spotted with cyclists, joggers, mums pushing prams, and old, dog-walking men, stretched in either direction. At some point the streetlamps clicked on, their warm gaze shadowed by whispering autumn leaves. How long had she been sitting there? Was she slipping away already?

The boulevard was empty, but Alex was unafraid. Her hand opened and closed. Closed and opened. And then, a touch. Gentle but constant as his hand slipped into hers. He didn't say anything, just pulled her to her feet, and they walked as the leaves swelled but did not fall.

He did not speak, but she heard him.

I know.

Old Woman in a Black Buick
Tripping on Nine Inch Nails

One hand on the wheel, the other on the gun, she drove the Buick down I-80 cranking Nine Inch Nails, volume high as she. A rosary dangling from the rear-view – shadow swinging like a hung man on the sun-shrivelled dash – reminded her of Chuck.

They'd met in a bar in Omaha. She had no money, but she did have tits. He had plenty of the former, not enough of the latter. It was a fuck made in heaven. He was half her age and twice her height, but none of that mattered lying down. She'd wrecked his marriage, then his head, snatched his stash and his car, then headed for California.

She pulled in for gas outside Salt Lake. The attendant was mid-fifties, but sun and snow had burnt him old. After he filled her tank, she followed him into the empty station.

'Blow or blowie?' she said.

One look at her tits and 'Blowie,' was all he said.

She stopped off in Reno before hitting the Sierras; undid a few buttons; slapped tits and her last twenty bucks on a blackjack table. Five hours later, she was five grand up and under the dealer in a comped suite shoving a pinkie up his ass. He finished first but finished her off even though break time was over and fucking guests was against the rules.

Her kinda guy. She thought about hanging around as she emptied the minibar – danced around the room, tits flapping, ass pumping – then passed out.

Next day she snorted the rest of the stash and hit the Sierras around noon. A trucker drew up; stared down from his cab. She undid her halter top with one deft hand, flipped him a tit and then the bird. She was over the pass and going down fast. Hand on the gun, she rolled down the window and shot at the truck.

'Fuck you, fucker trucker! Fuck you. Fuck me. Fuck cancer! Fuck it all!'

She took her foot off the brake, pumped up the volume and went down screaming.

Thoughts While Being Strangled on Honeymoon

This is not happening.

This is not happening.

I LOVE you.

This is not happening. This is not happening. I love you. This is not happening... This is not happening? This is not happening?? This is not HAPPENINGTHIS IS NOT HAPPENINGTHISISNOT happening is not happening!!! This is not happening ILOVEYOU This is not happeningThis is not happeninhisnohap is not is not not

not

h a p p e n I n g.

This...

is...

not...

I

Love

You

This

is

not

Love

The Bar of Chocolate

No longer are there first times, only last. Krista sits, fingers folded, at a narrow table, the hard wood splintered by time and tears. A thousand, thousand tears.

To either side of her, a man reclines as if waiting for a barmaid to deliver a tankard and mount his lap. The scents from their uniforms are wet wool, gunpowder, and the peculiar odour of disdain excreted when man no longer acknowledges his enemy as human.

The women before them are naked, harvested of all their jewels—clothes, gold, hair, fillings. They shiver but do not beg. What is the point? What will be done, will be done. No one can do anything about it, not even Krista.

Krista has a headache from their smell. Not sweat but the stench of fear like crushed roses. Something stirs in her at the sight of the child peering from the loop of her mother's right arm. She pushes the feeling away; it cannot be allowed to fester.

Men hunt to survive, blood-stained by necessity. To eat. To protect – kill the vermin who threaten; save our people from the pestilence which would destroy us. Some take pleasure in the kill. Krista has seen the flush of their cheeks, the rapid, low pant; the gleam of cold sweat on their brow. She neither enjoys nor regrets it, only understands the necessity.

The women are many, while behind the desk, only three. Why do they not rise? Fight? Ghosts with wraith-like limbs, in the hollow of their eyes, Krista sees shadows sunk beyond despair into acceptance.

They wait.

The commandant calls forth the little girl. The mother's arm tightens in a rictus of defiance.

'I mean no harm.' He smiles; gestures with a bar of chocolate saved for the children. Those few who are left.

When the commandant pushes the chocolate bar in front of Krista, she knows what to do. She has watched the scene play out a hundred times. She looks at the chocolate – the deep, rich colour, like earth. Earth, mud, mines, diamonds. They've robbed us of our country, our heritage, our rights. This is not a child but the spawn of restitution.

'What is your name, little girl?' Krista is pretty, her eyes kind. Blonde hair loose and cascading on her shoulders, she must look like an angel to those before her.

The girl peeks out, looks to her mother who can only nod. Why not give the child one brief instant of joy? The men tense beside her, their trousers bulge. To rob life is nothing – common, banal. But to steal joy, hope? That is power.

'Sophie.' The girl's voice is broken as if words are foreign to her language of tears.

Smiling, Krista picks up the bar and rises. The tool of her beauty has gotten her far. It both soothes and provokes depending on the slant of her smile. She moves to the other side of the table. The mother stiffens, looks Krista in the eye, and for an instant, a fire burns within.

Krista's smile does not falter as she crouches, eyes now level with the girl. She breaks off a piece, and pungent fragrance fills the room like sprayed perfume. 'You are a good girl, Sophie. We have heard such wonderful things,' Krista says and holds out the bar. 'This is your reward, my darling. Take it.'

The girl cannot resist. A string of hair catches in a bubble of drool at the corner of her mouth and Krista's fingers twitch to pinch it.

Reaching tentatively, the girl steps from the umbrella of her mother. Tiny hand trembling with fear's might, she takes the thick chocolate and grasps it in her dirty hands. Looks to her mother – to bring it to her, to share.

'No, my darling. It is all for you,' Krista says. The girl's eyes shine. How old is she? Seven? Eight? Old enough to have known kindness. Young enough to still trust.

The child takes it, and the room stills, the crowd fearful of setting anything in motion. Perhaps they still hope. Hope is always the last thing to die.

The crunch when she bites, Krista hears it now. The soft moan of pleasure which sighs from the girl's mouth. She doesn't chew but lets it linger, savouring the flavour fumes, the rich lacquer of sweetness.

The joy. That pure moment. Krista sees it in her eyes; has both the power to give and to take it away. She pulls the gun from her boot and shoots the girl in the head before she can take another bite. The girl falls to the dusty floor, eyes still open and gleaming.

The screams are quickly silenced by the other two officers. All except the mother who stands trembling, surrounded by a sea of bodies, eyes darting between her daughter and the two men. She neither screams nor cries as they take her, only seeks to reach for her daughter and touch her one last time.

Krista watches because she must. She does not enjoy it but cannot look away. When the men are done, she must end it. The woman's eyes are open, her head turned to the left where her dead daughter lies. She does not move. Krista is quick. She does not enjoy what she must do but understands it must be done. Before the war, she refused to kill anything, even insects. But it is different now. Everything is different.

The commandant offers no explanation, no excuse. Krista knows by now – I am human; they are not. Cattle. Worse, swine. No, vermin to be eradicated before they destroy me and mine.

The floor tiles are red. Good planning? Or serendipity? This is the way Krista now thinks. She is not sad and feels no remorse. Once, she worried what this made her. Now, she no longer cares.

She loosens the little girl's fingers, pries the chocolate from her rigid hand.

It is treacly with blood.

The Shutters

'Do you remember...?' It was always Jonathan's first question. Otherwise he never knew where to begin.

'Don't ask me that.'

His brother Charles sat in a comfortable chair at the side of the bed, hands folded neatly in his lap where the nurse had placed them. Morning sunshine bounced off the white walls but never quite reached him. Charles blinked. 'Close the shutters. The light hurts my eyes.'

Jonathan stood, kicking an old suitcase that jutted from under the bed. It was the only thing in Charles' corner that was not hospital issue. That and the threadbare, stuffed monkey that held court on his pillow. Jonathan closed the shutters, then lifted the monkey.

Jonathan tried again, monkey dangling from his hand as if from a branch. 'I remember the time we went to Africa. Grandpa had come to stay in the spare bedroom. He was as old as we were young and couldn't remember much, only the war in Africa. Every night he told us stories.'

Charles sat in shadow, head bald as the old monkey's, a jagged scar stitched across his forehead.

'We snuck Grandpa's suitcase from under his bed. Pulled out pilot goggles and caps, even his old RAF rucksack. Put everything on, squished ourselves into the suitcase and pretended it was a plane. We were going to fly to Africa to bring Monkey home.'

A solitary tear beaded in the corner of Charles' eye. His finger twitched towards Monkey.

'I remember,' he said.

The Whole of the Moon

It hurt like hell, but she let him do it anyway. She'd do anything to get him back. Even that.

All her friends said it was futile. Hell, even the marriage counsellor told them to get a divorce.

It only made her want him more.

He videoed the whole thing with his phone. She let him do that, too. Put on a show even. Give him something to watch in the flat he'd rented above the chippy back in Killarney. Keep him from looking elsewhere.

'Have you fucked anyone?' she said, pulling up her stockings. Slow, like her tongue had been.

'That's none of your business. We're separated.'

'We're still married.' Thank God, Ireland made you wait four years for a divorce.

He adjusted himself, looked up. 'No, I haven't.'

He talked to the driver on the way over. She stared out the window at the narrow streets of Cork; flashed back to college piss-ups and heels broken on cobblestone paths. Why had she ever dropped out of uni to marry him? Her phoned beeped – a text from their eldest wondering where the brown sauce was. Yeah, she gave it all up for that. She sighed. What the hell would she have done with an arts degree anyway?

'Oh my God, look, a circus.' Mouth open, she scrambled out of the taxi without paying and gaped at the enormous blue and yellow striped tent.

He tossed the driver a twenty and walked over to her. 'Like our marriage,' he said. The fading sun spotlighted him at just the wrong angle. He'd gained as much weight drinking as she'd lost on her diet of heartbreak and Valium. For the first time in ages, more fellas were sizing her up than women him.

'Ha. Ha.'

'You do know that's why they call it Live at the Marquee, right?'

She ignored that and instead, pointed to a giant Ferris wheel turning behind shivering trees, 'A fun fair too.' He loved roller coasters and anything that knocked the breath out of him, including her, once upon a time.

'Do I look okay?' she said, brushing down her dress as they entered the courtyard.

'You look fine.' He handed her a pint in a plastic cup, and she had an overwhelming urge to crush it over his head and shower him in Heineken.

We struggled for years while you went back to college to upskill. You got your fancy new job and car and walked out, leaving me with a mountain of debt and despair. I gave you everything. Took nothing. I hate you. I fucking hate you.

'Thanks,' was all she said.

A few more pints and they relaxed into the music. When she leaned back into him, he stiffened, but then 'Whole of the Moon' began, and his arms slide round her like all their yesterdays. She closed her eyes, and he was her knight in shining armour once more. College might have gotten her out of the hellhole she called home, but he had taught her love was more than fists and fright.

It didn't take much convincing to get him to the fair after. She hated every ride but gagged back vomit and rode the wall of death with him.

'I'm not going on any Ferris wheel,' he said. 'I'd have to talk to you.'

'That's harsh.'

'Do you want me to lie?'

Once in a while, yes. Wasn't that what marriage was all about?

The Ferris wheel perched on the banks of the River Lee. He sat as far from her as he could. 'For balance.'

At that late hour there weren't many passengers, and the going round was slow going. They dangled for some time at the top. Her stomach had settled enough for her to appreciate the twinkling lights and shining moon.

'It's whole,' she said.

'What?'

'The moon, silly. It's whole.'

'Not quite. Think it's supposed to be full in a couple of days.'

She unbuckled her safety harness. What good was that thin chain anyway?

'What are you doing?' he said as she sat next to him, car swaying.

She touched his face like a teenager trying to cop a feel. The diamond on her finger was small but still glittered in the moonlight, full or not.

He jerked away. 'I know what you're playing at. We're not getting back together.'

'I know you still love me.' But she was back in 2002 when he'd taken her to Cork for their anniversary, and they'd sat on a bench by the river, his jacket on her shoulders, her face in his chest and he'd sang to her and even though it was half-covered with clouds, they'd both seen the whole damn moon.

'That's not enough.'

'Of course, it is.

'I'm tired of paying for what your parents did to you. I've been paying for twenty years.'

'What are you talking about?'

He sighed. 'You know exactly what I'm talking about.'

He made no move to stop her as she stepped to the edge of the tub. It jerked dangerously, but she didn't attempt to hold on. Below, the Lee glittered like the rock on her finger, the moon above, his eyes when he'd fucked her for the last time.

If she jumped just far enough she should reach the river. She didn't know much about physics but hoped the splash would cover him in water. Dirty, filthy water just like the bath they'd nearly drowned her in. If he stood, crawled over, tried to stop her, she'd push him instead. See where leaving her got him.

'I'm sorry. I do love you.' Just what her father would say after he'd beaten her. 'I just can't. Not anymore. One of us has to be happy.'

She took off her ring and threw it. The moonlight caught the stone, and it twinkled like a distant, dying star. The splash it made was small but definite as it sunk into the dirty water.

'You're right. I want a divorce.'

Wild Grass

For Jean-Michel Nicolier (1966-1991)

He does not have the eyes of war. Wide and brown. Smiling. Poised between youth and manhood. Waiting.

On the news, Vukovar – a city under siege – crumbles like sandcastles in the tide on the banks of the Danube.

'These people need help,' he says.

Maman folds back the page of her book and places it on the lace-covered table. Makes dinner – coq au vin, his favourite – and sets it before him. He sniffs but continues staring at the screen.

'You do not even speak the same language,' she says.

'There is only one language in war. Listen.'

On the television, the city screams.

He kisses her cheek. 'I'll return, Maman, I promise. You know I'm a wild grass that never goes away.' He eats, eyes wide. Gleaming.

The next and last time Maman sees him, it is on the television. Arms wrapped around a gun, smiling as the bombs shriek. His eyes – dark, haunted – his eyes are the eyes of war. His mouth forms words – *je t'aime, Maman* is what she hears.

His remains are never found, but upon the field where he and three hundred others fell, nothing ever grows.

Only wild grass.

White

The GP handed me a leaflet. 'Here's a list of foods to avoid. Oh, and a script for folic acid. You need to be taking that every day. The Royal will send you an appointment to see the consultant at eight weeks, then another at twenty...'

He kept talking, but my attention had already flown – across borders, time zones and five years. Back to the specialist clinic in San Francisco. The bitter, white walls and lab coats. The four scans by three experts. My first husband's warm fingers on my cold arm...

'I'm sorry, Sarah, but your choices are limited. You can carry the baby to term, but it will die at birth. Or you can terminate the pregnancy now.'

The pregnancy? A second ago, it was my baby.

'You must decide soon. You can't go much longer if you choose to terminate.'

My baby. Too small to punch but big enough to wave, I felt the flutters in my belly, against my hand. My clammy hand. I shouldn't have sat in the sauna so long. Not had that glass of wine, that last cigarette. That abortion. I killed my first baby, and God would take his due. I stared at the white walls, the bright lights. The judgement in their eyes. Choked on snot and denial.

This time would be different.

I took the Bounty pack of coupons and advice booklet from the GP with limp hands, went home and read about all the things that could hurt my baby: soft cheese; peanuts; liver and vitamin A; raw fish and shellfish; raw or undercooked, unpasteurized eggs or milk; cat litter – germs.

I opened my cupboards. The fridge. Started throwing things out. The greasy, white clock over the cooker tick-tocked. I took it down and washed it.

That night I dreamt of the hospital gurney clang, clanging down the corridor. Sheets, military tight. The disgust in the nurse's eyes. *Don't look at me that way. Why are you looking at me that way? I don't want my baby to die.* The drugs doing their business – pulsing lights above, stars in the ceiling panels. *There's no heaven for murdered babies.* I sobbed, 'Please, oh, God. Please. My baby.' Clutched at the nurse with my one loose hand. She shrugged me away.

Three a.m., I woke, sheets memory tentacles around me. Screaming.

The smell hit me – like the stench of black blood that dribbled from me for weeks after. My baby's blood. My dead baby. It was the mould which crept from the single-glazed windows like mutant spider legs. The back of peeling wallpaper black with the stuff. I ripped it down, scraping stubborn strips with a maxed-out credit card. Bleach straight, I scrubbed the walls white. Scrubbed the flat until my skin wept.

Stared at my hands, bleached white, and raw.

Ice-Cream Man

It was Friday. John had worked hard all week doing a job few others would. He came home, ate the dinner his wife put before him – pork chops on Fridays; had a beer in front of the telly. Snoozed.

Ding-ding-a-ling.

He jumped up; checked his pockets. The screen door slammed behind him.

The neighbourhood kids were already lined up. Waiting. 'Hello, Mr Mason,' they said in unison.

'Hello, boys and girls. Everyone ready?'

They all nodded.

'Perfect! Who's first today?'

One by one, the children tip-toed to the van and placed their orders – a 99 here, a bar there, a few ice-cream sandwiches, even a slushie or two. They thanked him with milk-frothy grins. John ordered a cone with chocolate sprinkles and paid for the lot. He opened his mouth wide and slurped the twisty tail of vanilla ice cream on top.

'Excuse me, Mr Mason?'

John turned to find two policemen. 'Yes, officers?' he said.

'Did you purchase ice cream for all these children?'

John looked around. The children were laughing as they skipped down the street. Their parents, however, stood in their front gardens, arms crossed and frowning.

'Yes,' John said. 'I buy the neighbourhood children an ice cream every Friday. Is there a problem?'

'Do you have permission from their parents?'

John frowned. 'No.'

'Would you mind coming down to the station with us, sir?'

John nodded and followed them to the police car. 'You can't bring that in the vehicle, sir,' one officer said, pointing at John's ice cream.

John dropped the cone. It began to melt as soon as it hit the tarmac.

*

John sat on a hard bench and stared at the STRANGER DANGER poster in the station. He thought back dozens of summers to when he was five and a half. Hottest day of the year and everyone was waiting for the ice-cream man. John was normally allowed one cone a week but had smiled another pound out of Mum. He got his usual, a vanilla cone with chocolate sprinkles. It was so hot the sprinkles slid down his hand before he could even take a bite.

Running to get inside before it melted altogether, he tripped and fell. The cone flew and landed with a sickening, PLOP. John tried to scoop it up but gathered tarmac pebbles instead of sprinkles. Tears burning his eyes, he ran back to the van.

'I'll wait five minutes for you to get some more money,' the ice-cream man said.

John ran home and emptied his piggy bank. Nothing but a few coppers. He pulled out the shiniest, spat on them, polished them against his shirt until they gleamed. Maybe the ice-cream man would think they were silver. John ran back, heart full of hope.

'Sorry, son,' said the ice-cream man.

John walked back to his dropped cone and cried as a dog licked it up. One by one, the other children and adults went past, each with a delicious ice cream, until finally, one stopped.

'Come on, John,' the man said. 'Let's get you another cone.'

Last Day of Summer

You wanted that toy, didn't you? Sure, it was only plastic, but its fifty parts clipped together in infinite combinations.

But he wouldn't give it to you, would he?

It's MINE!

Wouldn't even let you touch it. Didn't matter he already had five of them, one in every colour 'cause his parents were stinking rich and bought him anything and everything, even dug out their back garden and put in a swimming pool. Did he let you swim? Hell, no. He'd wave as he drifted by on that inflatable green crocodile. Tell you not to stick your bare feet in the cool, blue water 'cause the gators would get you.

SNAP! SNAP!

Sipping lemonade through a straw, hat low over his eyes, feet trailing in the water, he didn't notice as you cracked the pieces apart. Nor when you threw them high in the air like tossing a bird back into the sky. He heard them though. The plop, plop like bird shit as they rained on the chlorinated water.

NOOOOO!

You laughed as he squealed but not out loud – on the inside where no one could hear and come running. You rooted for him as he tried to get them all. Egged him on, but he dived deep for that collectable red, glowing jewel which was heavy and sank fast. Just like him.

You held your breath...

The only thing you ever did together. Jumped in, clothes and all; dived straight to him, his eyes wide, unblinking; pried the red jewel from his clutched hand, smiled as the remaining pieces drifted down like autumn leaves.

The Pot of Black Gold

John stopped emptying the ashtray the day his fourth dog died. Made from glass – maybe even Waterford but as it was his Mum's and she was dead too, he couldn't ask her – it was heavy as his heart as he inhaled the first fumes of decay from Mackey's carcass.

He'd cleaned most of the blood, but brown crusts still wove in flaking ridges along the threadbare carpet. He lit a cigarette to clear the stench and stared at the delicate pyramid of fag ends in the thick-cut glass. The way he was smoking, it was a matter of days, hours even, before the whole thing collapsed upon itself like one of those Ponzi schemes where Mum had lost all the money. There was a special place in hell for those who preyed upon the ignorant and weak. A small, dark room, where their victims' hands reached through the walls to rip them apart. Piece by piece.

Of everyone he'd buried – three dogs, two wives, a parent and a child – John missed his mother the most. Thirty years gone now, she was. Lung cancer. He'd buried her on the hill, just like she wanted – palms crossed over a carton of Marlboro

Lights, under the one tree not broken by the angry Atlantic winds. One after the other, the rest had followed, and now Mackey would join them.

John had avoided it long as he could, but when the flies came that morning, on All Hallows' Eve, he knew it was time. Funny, that. Seeing flies so late in the year. Guess death drew them no matter the weather. Mackey lay in his favourite spot in front of the fireplace, except the fire had been cold for days now, and cold it would remain, just like Mackey. Though winter banged on the door demanding to be let in, John would never light another fire.

He stubbed out his fag and set about burying his dog.

Wet Atlantic gales filled the spaces in his joints where cartilage used to be with a permanent ache. John creaked and cracked as he lifted old Mackey in his arms, the innards shifting like one of those water beds he'd tried on a visit to San Francisco. That's where he'd met his first wife, Emily, a model and dancer. Pretty as a picture, she'd married him quick enough once she heard about his Irish castle. She did her duty and bore him three sons but then shrivelled in the isolation of the Kerry countryside. Turns out he couldn't buy everything she needed, though he tried. God knows he tried. Jackie, their eldest, found her swinging from a tree. Jackie had taken that hard; wasn't a year before he took his own life.

Mary from down the village had been his second wife. She'd lasted till the boys were reared and away to university then succumbed to the black tentacles of cancer rooted in her virgin womb. Now John was alone. His sons checked on him from time to time, but with Liam gone to Dublin and Jack over in the States, it wasn't very often. For ten years now, it had been just him and Mackey.

Why'd they have to kill him?

Blue tarp from the sheep shed lined the boot of John's old Volvo. Didn't have many sheep left either. Those bastards from Tralee had taken most of them. They drove down once a fortnight and filled their white van in the night. The Guards were no help, and what was John to do on his own? Mackey had tried though. He was a good dog, Mackey was. Until they'd knifed him.

The car jerked and shuddered as John worked his way down the drive. It hadn't been paved since Mary died and now, like his heart, was mostly holes. Clouds boiled overhead, and the Atlantic rumbled in response. He'd better hurry; he didn't fancy digging in a storm.

The wind whistled warning through bare branches as John lifted Mackey from the boot. He chose a spot near Mary as she'd picked Mackey from the litter before she died. Confined to her bed, Mackey had licked the face off Mary and hadn't he whined for a week once she passed.

The old wood moaned and groaned like John's joints as he thrust the shovel into the hard ground, the earth black-gold and pungent from all the dead things buried there. By the time he was done, as much sweat as rain was lashing off him. John laid Mackey, tarp and all, in the cold ground, said a short prayer and covered him with earth. As he tapped the mound with his heel, a queer tingling ran up and down John's spine.

He paused in his work and listened to the rumble of an approaching vehicle.

He walked back to the car and pulled the rifle from the boot. When the white van pulled up seconds later, he was ready.

Yellow

She was yellow with fear. Cold piss ran through her veins instead of hot down her leg. This was no Marvel superhero movie where she could sprout wings and loop the fuck out of there. Though she wished it was. Wished it was. Wishes are fishes. Fishes are wishes.

'Fucking cop on yourself already for feck's sake,' Jimmy hissed, breath steaming like the train which had just left the station.

'That's the last train.' Mandy's voice trembled. They had missed it by seconds. Some fella with a belly of one too many pints and a heart attack waiting to happen had tried to stick his hand in the gap to hold it open, eyes big as his belly. He knew. Oh yes, he knew.

Jimmy ignored the display blinking NOT IN SERVICE. NOT IN SERVICE. 'It fucking isn't.'

But they were alone on the platform.

'It's like that movie. Warriors. Warriors. Come out and play. Remember, Jimmy? Remember?'

'Yeah, I wish homicidal gangs were our worst problem.'

Mandy wrapped her piss cold arms around herself. 'There's no way out now.'

Jimmy held her as the red tail lights of the train disappeared around the tunnel bend. 'Doesn't matter. Where the fuck they gonna go, anyway?'

'End of the line. End of the line for everyone,' Mandy giggled.

Jimmy dropped his arms and for the first time looked at her as a liability.

'Don't you leave me, Jimmy Murphy. Don't you fucking leave me.' Her voice rose with every syllable. She could see him weighing his options. It only took a second or two. Didn't matter they'd been together for five years, an abortion, his brother's suicide and a trial. None of that mattered now. Nothing mattered...

He grabbed her hand and pulled. 'Come on. I know a way out.'

'But where we gonna go, Jimmy? Where we gonna go?'

He didn't answer, just ran. She had no choice but to follow.

They made it to the surface and darkness. It was quiet as a nightmare before the monster pounces. The alarm clock of Mandy's pounding heart wouldn't slow. They'll find us now. Find us for sure.

But the streets were Christmas-dawning empty.

No more Christmases. Not ever. Ever. Can't go home. There were no homes anyway. Only cells. They were gathering them up, slamming the doors and throwing away the keys. Mandy felt the window eyes watching. The curtains twitching. Was it better to be locked up waiting for the food to run out? For everyone to turn on each other? For mothers to eat their young?

What would you do, Mandy? Would you eat Jimmy? Would ya? Huh?

'I know where there's a boat.' Jimmy said as they crouched behind some bins. Where were the rats? Surely, they would inherit the earth along with the cockroaches?

'We're too far from the water, Jimmy. We'll never make it.'

'Bullshit,' Jimmy said, and they started running again.

The air slap-dashed against their faces as they ran through mist that had either fallen from the charcoal sky or risen from the ground like huffing and puffing corpses dragging themselves from hell. It's a nightmare, right? All just a nightmare. I'm gonna wake up, Jimmy by my side and we'll have a smoke and laugh about it. He'll tell me I'm a psycho and better lay off the drugs, but I stopped that shit years ago so what the fuck is this now?

'Mandy.' Jimmy panted and heaved, but his voice was full of something both had forgotten. Hope.

The pier was empty. Not a sailboat, yacht or cargo ship in sight. Maybe the mist had swallowed them whole.

'Are we dead, Jimmy? Is that it? Are we dead and just don't know it yet?'

Jimmy laughed. 'You edjit. Look.'

She followed his finger to the dinghy lap dancing against the pier. The tide was high, and all they had to do was step into it and push off.

Thank Christ. She'd never believed in God, but someone or something was looking out for them. Drawn Jimmy through the fog to the pier. Saved a boat, a small boat but big enough for the two of them to hold hands and sail into the sunset. There's no sun, stupid. Haven't seen that fucker for ten days. Ha ha, days. Ten whatever the fuck, now.

There was no motor, so Mandy lay back while Jimmy did the rowing.

'Is it getting warmer, Jimmy?' she said five minutes or five hours later. Hard to tell in unshifting twilight.

'You fucking joking?' Jimmy said, sweat lashing from his forehead. 'You lying there like a princess and me killing myself here.'

'A princess you rescued. I love you, Jimmy.'

Jimmy grunted.

It was then Mandy noticed the water. 'We got a leak, Jimmy. Oh fuck. The boat's got a leak.'

Jimmy drew in the oars. 'Look for something. Something to bleeding shove in the hole.'

But there was nothing.

'Jesus, Jimmy. It's like bathwater. Like a sauna. Like a lie down after a hard day's work and someone's rubbing the job out of your muscles and I'm just going to lie back in it for a bit. Float like. Jimmy?'

But Jimmy was already lying next to her. Steam rising from him like a train through the night. If only we'd caught the train. If only...

Mandy started leaking. What harm? Everyone pissed in the sea. As the water turned yellow like spices in a soup, she felt herself fading, eyelids like sinking ships, and luxuriating in the warmth.

'Christ, Jimmy, I can't remember the last time I felt this warm. This good. Jimmy?'

But Jimmy was a thought. A memory through a sieve as Mandy cooked in the hot water. He was her last thought and it was a good one.

She never even felt the spear pierce her flesh.

Brandy

It was no longer possible to walk to the end of Miller's Pier. Sun, sea and time had weathered the wooden pillars and planks to pale silver husks. Harsh, New England winters had done the rest, claiming more and more of the once robust structure until one of the planks disintegrated under Samantha Burke and sent her plummeting.

Brandy had seen the whole thing. Samantha flailing like a harpooned shark on the stake of wood. It was neither quick nor painless. Sometimes, late at night, the sea-blasted wind howled along the boardwalk like her cries, scaring the teenagers who made out in the sand.

The council hadn't deemed Miller's Pier worthy of repair – for at least ten years, all boats had been moored in the town harbour, so its use was limited to the odd fisherman and kids who dived off it in summer and drank on it in winter. Some unsightly boards and fencing were banged up until the residents in their million-dollar, beach-front properties kicked up a fuss at the eyesore.

'So, now they're pulling the whole thing down.' Brandy told the guy as they walked along the boardwalk. She didn't know his name. Didn't want to. He wasn't listening anyway. The only thing he was paying attention to was her tits, so Brandy didn't mention the part about how she had pushed Samantha.

The guy whipped his head around. 'What's that?'

'It's just the wind. But some say it's the ghost of Samantha Blake.'

'Who?'

'Never mind.' Brandy sat on the edge of the boardwalk to take off her sneakers, undoing another button on her sweater in the process. She wasn't wearing anything underneath, not even a bra. Bet he noticed that.

He pulled her up and tried to shove his tongue down her throat. Yep, he noticed.

'Not here.' She nodded at the streetlights and nearby houses where canned applause from *The Late, Late Show* drifted through open windows.

He kept one hand rough on her arm and adjusted himself with the other. 'Where then?'

Jesus, he really was an idiot. She took his hand and drew him down the boardwalk. 'Somewhere more private.'

The weather-beaten planks ended at the last house. Beyond was marshland. A few years back, a banker named Martin Turner, keen on a shorefront address, had filled in a plot and built the biggest house in town. For a week. Luckily he'd taken the wife and three kids to town for dinner, so they hadn't sunk with the house. Brandy had been walking with another guy and saw the whole thing. It's how she got the idea.

'Do you have a boat?' she said.

'Huh? A boat?'

'Yeah, a boat. It's the seaside. A lot of people do. My grandfather had one. He called it the Apex.'

'Apex? What's that mean?' At least he was trying to pay attention now.

'It means the highest part of something.' Brandy said and stopped. This was the spot – she'd tied a yellow ribbon around one of the reeds to mark it.

'Seems an odd name for a boat.' He pulled her into the reeds where not even the moon could find them, unzipped his pants and waited.

'It wasn't the boat he was referring to.' Brandy said and pushed.

She felt no hatred for the guy as she watched him sink. It was slow, and he screamed a good bit. She'd have to do something about that next time. A tense two minutes until the muck seeped into his gurgling mouth and silenced him for good.

No one came to investigate.

Brandy untied the yellow ribbon and returned to the sand. Staring out across the water, she thought of her grandfather; how he loved to sail. He'd take his granddaughters out for 'special' trips. It had always been a treat.

Until he began to rape them.

The cops bought her story about Grandpa slipping on the wet deck and falling overboard. She was a tiny slip of a thirteen-year-old. What else could they think?

Brandy stood at water's edge and looked out over the Sound. It was around this spot Grandpa's body had washed up on the shore, tangled in seaweed and half-eaten by fish. Samantha had held her hand as the police examined the scene. If Brandy regretted anything, it was telling Samantha the truth. Who would have thought her best friend would threaten to betray her?

Brandy buttoned her sweater against the night. She'd always loved the water: each wave a fingerprint; the foam white as the tears of angels. Nothing withstood its inexorable tide, not even regret.

Sex Life – Part Two

Thank God for the internet. She's watched more porn than a horny teenager with a perpetual boner. Her kids, hell, her grandkids would be mortified if they knew. Click. Click. Category after category – mature, old/young, big tits, threesome, lesbian, gangbang, public, MILF – she needs something different. That elusive spark that would finish her off in no time because her fingers are a bit arthritic and her wrist aches if she's at it for too long.

Sometimes, memories are enough. She'd been quite a looker in her day – had her fair share of men and the odd woman or two. Tits were always a tad shite but her legs and arse, they had been something. Still were to be fair, but all the floppy bits were a bit off-putting.

So, she doesn't look.

Instead she lies back on the bed – duvet bunched under her ass to tilt it just right, elbow resting on a cushion – and opens her legs. Closes the laptop, then her eyes. Settles upon her last lover. Young. Fit. Filthy. She takes his hard cock in her wet mouth but not for long 'cause he wants her, wants her bad. He loved her ass. Loved it a bit too much – gave her a haemorrhoid.

She grimaces, shifts against the duvet, thinks of...

A bar – dark, dank, musty. In the one toilet, she's banged up against the wall, thick hands holding her tight, his breath all nicotine and panting moans against her neck. He fiddles under her skirt. Squeezes. Rips off her panties, throws them on the floor. Jesus, it's mucky in here – feet sticking, and, God help me, my arse better not touch that wall. Where the fuck's the condom, and where has his cock been? In another woman?

There was a woman once...

Fleshy. Soft on top of her; grinding the coffee; tongue tickling her tits. Hands squeezing. She threads her hands through that thick red hair, pulls her closer...

Closer.

Closer.

Nothing.

She groans. Opens the laptop back up and presses play. Gets a message:

'Error: No Connection'.

Joe

Joe drove a truck for his old man. I'd never been in the cab of a truck and thought it would be fun to tag along for the day.

'It's not very comfortable,' he said, trying to dissuade me and he was right, but I didn't care. I was nineteen and could bend my long legs at odd angles so shovelled them under the bulbous dash without complaint.

He put a tape in the player, then the truck in gear.

'Who's this?' I said, turning it up, the sound all echoes and angst.

'The Teardrop Explodes. They're from Liverpool.'

'Like The Beatles,' I said.

'Nothing like them.'

'Just like the city is nothing like the state,' I said, snow flurries splattering on the window like tiny bombs. When you grew up in Connecticut, New York always meant the city. Upstate was just an extension of New England and in winter that meant dead things and snow.

It was a long drive, and my legs were cramped by the time we passed security at the gate and drove down the long, manicured drive to the hospital. I wanted nothing more than to get out and stretch while Joe unloaded the delivery.

'Don't get out of the truck,' he said as he backed into the loading bay. He wore sunglasses against the snow glare, so I couldn't read if he was serious or not.

I looked around. Nothing but a bunch of Christmas trees festooned with snow. 'Come on, my legs are killing me.'

'Don't. It's dangerous.'

I laughed.

'I mean it, Sarah. Don't let appearances fool you. This is a high-security mental hospital.

'Aren't they locked up?'

'The most dangerous are but still, stay in the truck.'

I could hear him talking to some fellas and unloading, but after a while everything was quiet. Snow began to pile on the windscreen, and the cab went coffin-like. I stared at the door handle. Was reminded of the time I was six, and the babysitter told me not to open the front door because her puppy would run into traffic and get killed. How I knew what would happen but twisted the doorknob anyway and the dog bolted – the screeching brakes, the thump. The poor thing crawling back up the stairs at my feet.

They had to shoot it.

I looked around. There was no one or nothing, and I had to piss. I put my hand on the door handle.

A face appeared at the window.

I screamed bloody murder, but it didn't go away, just grinned. It could have been a woman, but the mad hair and

Invasion of the Body Snatcher eyes made it hard to tell – her pupils were tiny as a pinprick and just as sharp.

She jangled the handle. Pulled as I struggled to hold it closed. I was losing ground and starting to panic when Joe and a few other fellas pulled her away, kicking and witch-cackling.

'Christ, that was scary,' I said as Joe climbed into the cab and locked the doors. I lit a cigarette with trembling hands. 'Her eyes. What the fuck was wrong with her eyes, Joe?'

'It's the drugs,' he said.

'Drugs? What kind of drugs do that to your eyes?'

'The strongest ones.' He lowered his sunglasses and turned to me. It was only for a second, but that's all it took. The ink of his pupils had constricted to a black hole.

'What did you do, Joe?'

He wouldn't answer. Not until we pulled into a truck stop just over the state line. We sat across from each other in the diner. He flipped the levers of the tabletop jukebox while we waited for my food and Joe's coffee. 'Nothing but shit,' he said.

I stared at him. Waited.

'I'm a heroin addict,' he said like telling me the time of day.

'What?'

'Heroin. I take heroin.'

Heroin was only something in the movies. 'I don't believe you.'

He looked around, shrugged off his leather and rolled up his sleeve. 'See these?' He pointed at some red, angry-looking dots that I'd always thought were infected mosquito or flea bites. 'That's where I stick the needle in.'

I rubbed my finger over the angry holes, willing them to vanish. The waitress came over with the coffee pot. Joe jerked away and rolled down his sleeves.

'How long?' I said once the waitress left. She'd probably seen everything there was to see and had taken no notice of Joe.

'Not long, I tried it for the first time a few weeks ago.'

'Stop.'

'I can't.' His hands twitched as he lit a cigarette. He wouldn't look at me. 'I don't want to.'

The diner shrunk and stilled. 'Why? What's it like?'

His eyes went all far-away. 'It's the best feeling in the world. Better than sex. Better than anything.'

I winced at that. 'I want to try it.'

He looked at me then. Stared me straight in the eye. 'No.'

'Why not? If it's the best feeling ever... let me see what it's like. Just once.' But it was more than that. It was jealousy pure and simple.

'Not even once.'

'But...'

'No.' He slammed his hand on the table right next to mine. A few of the truckers looked over but long as he wasn't beating me, they were going to mind their own business.

His fingers crawled over, took mine in his. 'I love you, Sarah.' The words came slow as if each one brought him closer to a trapdoor. 'Promise me one thing.'

My heart paused while my mind raced. I wanted to go to a club, dance like a lunatic then fuck him clean. 'Anything,' I said.

'You'll never try it.'

I took his hand. Stilled it. Nodded.

Three Is a Magic Number

Martin Hayes didn't know what was more unusual – twenty degrees of sunshine during mid-term break or the stranger who'd pitched a fold-up table in front of the end-of-terrace wall. You never saw one nor the other in Hightown.

If that wasn't odd enough, with his black suit, fridge-white shirt and bow-tie, the stranger was a disturbing blend of undertaker and ice-cream man. Except he wasn't selling anything nice as ice cream. Going by the empty table, he wasn't selling anything at all. He sat on a lawn chair, arms resting on the table, fingers laced, thumbs twiddling. Waiting for what?

Mystery had left Martin's life long ago, swept away by the brush of middle-aged routine, yet he paused long enough to wonder and with that came the need for answers.

'Hello,' Martin said.

The man rose and offered his hand. 'Hello.'

Martin had seen his fair share of junkies and whores and was well used to hands of decay, but there was something about the pale skin and ridged veins of the proffered hand that made him hesitate.

'What brings you to these parts?' Martin said, shivering as he took it.

'Nothing much.' The man's voice reminded him of his Mary when her lungs had gone paper-thin and sticky.

Martin tensed as the man reached into his breast-pocket, but all he pulled out was a business card and on it, two words: Three Wishes.

'Three wishes? What's that? A strip club?' He tried to laugh.

'If you want it to be.'

It was mid-day and quiet. A bit of wind picked up and whispered through a copse of leafy trees standing guard before a field where the local teens did drugs and each other.

'I don't mean to be rude...'

'Have you ever wanted something you could never have?'

Martin shrugged. 'Of course. Doesn't everyone?'

'Maybe, but not everyone gets the chance to have their wishes come true.' The stranger smiled. 'I'll make it easy for you, Martin.'

That's funny. I never told him my name.

'Play a little game with me, and I will grant you three wishes.'

Martin shuffled his feet. Time to move on, and fair play to the loon for staying out of the nuthouse for so long.

'You're sceptical. I don't blame you. Tell you what, I'll grant you one for free. Go on, Martin, make a wish. Doesn't have to be anything big.'

What harm? 'Okay,' Martin said. 'I wish I had a 99.' Easy enough, and he'd been wanting one ever since he'd seen the man.

'Done.'

Martin dropped the cone that appeared in his hand. 'How did you do that?'

'I grant wishes, Martin.'

Martin came to attention for the first time in ten years. 'What's the catch?'

The stranger glanced at the newspaper in Martin's hand, folded to the horses, bets ticked-off with red biro. 'I see you're a betting man.'

'Guess I am.'

The stranger reached into his pocket again. 'Don't be alarmed, I mean you no harm,' he said, pulling out a revolver and opening it to show Martin the chamber. 'There're three bullets evenly placed in nine chambers. I'm going to revolve the chamber so neither of us knows where the bullets are.'

Martin backed away. 'I don't think so.'

'Come now, Martin. You could have anything. Anything at all.'

Martin was stupored but not stupid. 'What's the catch?'

'No catch. Are you willing to take a small risk to reap huge reward?'

Mary. How he longed to see his Mary again. 'Mary. I want my Mary to be alive and healthy again.'

Then there she was, in the dress she'd been buried in, walking out of the trees, beautiful as the day he'd married her. Martin sucked his belly in and ran his fingers through his hair, but Mary stopped at the tree edge and came no closer.

'Not yet.' The stranger twirled the chamber and handed the gun to Martin. If he didn't do it quickly, it wouldn't be done at all. Martin put the gun to his head and pulled the trigger.

Click.

'Mary.' He ran to her. She smelled of sunshine and lavender. 'Mary. Mary. Mary.' He kissed her face a thousand times before the stranger coughed gently into his hand and checked his watch.

'Sorry to interrupt, but you must now make your other two wishes.'

'I don't want any more. One's enough for me.'

'I'm sorry, but that's not the bargain.'

'Fuck off.' Martin took two steps with Mary under his arm before a violent coughing fit overtook her, just like the ones from the cancer.

'I'm afraid I must insist.'

Martin took the gun from the stranger. 'I wish that none of these bullets hit me for the rest of my turns.' He said and pulled the trigger.

Click

As the bullet left the chamber, it jerked Martin's hand just enough that the bullet missed his head. Instead, it hit Mary standing right next to him.

'No.' Martin cried as Mary crumbled. 'No. Mary, no.' Martin picked up the gun and without thinking, said, 'I want my Mary,' and pulled the trigger.

Click.

Mary didn't stir from the puddle of blood coagulating on the concrete. Martin grabbed the stranger by the lapels and lifted him off the ground. 'You didn't keep your end of the bargain.'

'But you have your Mary.' The stranger said.

Martin put him down again. 'Don't make me bury her again.'

The stranger snapped his fingers, and the body was gone, but the blood remained. Martin continued down the path towards the bookies, leaving bloody prints as he went.

The Calm

For Chris

1986

Danny sings. Sings to Abi who settles back on pungent, dew-damp earth, stretches a slim arm, and points overhead.

'Look, Danny, the stars.'

Danny sings. Sings as the stars blink on one-by-one and the winter wheat whispers refrain.

Abi shivers and Danny shrugs off his jacket and covers her; strokes the side of her face. Abi's eyes are star bright, and he's mesmerized by the silent moons of her pupils, the worlds swimming in their seas.

'Don't stop, Danny. You sing so good. I could listen to you sing forever.'

All for you, Abi, he thinks but does not say. Instead, his second-biggest desire spills out in a rushing tumble, 'Come with me, Abi. Please. There's nothing for us here, only each other.'

Abi takes his rough farm hand in her soft one, 'I gotta take care of Poppa, Danny. You know that.'

Danny sighs. Takes a breath for that star-high note he's been trying to reach, opens his mouth to swallow summer breeze fuel, but the air has stilled. No wheat rustle. No cricket chirps. A heavy weight pushes down from the sky. In the distance, Old Man Jerome's cows grumble.

'Abi!' Danny pulls her up. 'The Calm!'

Breath held, eyes wide, it's eternity before God bowling thunder rumbles in the distance. They head towards the road where lightning stabs the horizon and a star-blotting cloud funnels from the sky.

'Twister, Abi. Run! Run!'

Danny's house is closer but still not at all, so they head for Old Man Jerome's. Dust, ozone, whittled wheat and something not of this world but visiting, swoosh thick as the wind pushes through the Calm and gives chase.

They reach the cellar two steps before their last breath and scramble into darkness. The roar is locomotive loud as the twister tears across the plain. Abi clings to the anchor of Danny's arms, and even though he knows she can't hear him, Danny whispers in her ear, 'I'll protect you, Abi. Forever and always.'

1996

Abi sits at the kitchen table, husband's hand on her shoulder, and writes:

Dear Danny,

Don't send me any more letters. I'm married now. To Tom.

Tears pooling, Abi pauses until Tom squeezes, digging his nails under her shoulder blade.

I don't love you anymore, Danny. Never did. I love Tom. He and I, we've got two kids. He was here for me when you weren't. Now, you leave me alone. You hear? Go sing your songs.

Abi looks up at Tom who nods. She signs the letter, spilled teardrop dotting the i, and hands it over to him. Watches as he takes all Danny's letters and feeds them to the stove, one by one.

Out on the front porch, wood warm under bare feet, Abi cups her cheekbone as it bruises black.

'Forever and always,' she whispers as the stars blink on.

2006

Danny sings. Sings to a faceless, chanting crowd. The bigger he's gotten, the further away his fans are. He misses the days he could reach out and shake hands. Now, there's only a line of security guards and a sea of camera lights blinking like stars in the night sky.

Danny sings. Sings of all he's wrought. He's got houses but no home; lovers but no love.

Over the thunder of stomping feet, the chant of DAN-EE, DAN-EE, DAN-EE, he hears a voice, clear as if inside his head. Stage left is the girl he met at last night's gig, biting her bottom lip. It's been a million years since he's heard that voice, but he'd know it anywhere, and it's not her.

The clamour of the crowd silences; the band fades away. Danny hears nothing, not even the roar of his own held breath as everything stills in the Calm.

Forever and Always, Danny Matthews.

Danny places his guitar in its stand as the band grumbles and his manager gestures wildly. He walks straight off stage, gets in his car and hits the road. It's nearly twenty-two hours to Lincoln. He'll do it in fifteen. He lowers the top of his Mustang, blue like her eyes.

'I'm coming, Abi. Hold on, baby, I'm coming.'

2006

Abi pumps the shotgun with her one good arm. Points it at Tom's head. She's not crying and never will again. Tom's the one who's crying now.

She hears the car pull up, assumes it's the cops but doesn't turn.

'Don't do it, Abi. He's not worth it,' Danny says.

'You don't know what he's done, Danny,' she says, still not turning. She thinks of her two boys who moved away. How they never visit or call. How they'll never speak to her again.

Danny's close now, close enough for her skin to goose-bump. Doesn't matter. Nothing else matters but putting the bastard in the ground.

Danny's hand is on the barrel of the gun, and all Abi can do is look in his eyes as the world calms. He touches the side of her face, and she lets him take it.

'Get yourself in the car, Abi,' Danny says. 'There's nothing here for you now.'

Danny looks at the shotgun. At Tom. Thinks about it twice before emptying the shells and punching that asshole in the face. Hard.

The sky is dark but spilling light as they hit the road. Danny puts his foot down on the pedal, and the wind collects Abi's wheat-coloured hair as they speed towards an endless horizon.

Forever and Always

Danny sings. Sings to Abi, grandbaby gurgling on her knee.

They're in California now, where the sea is never calm, but the sky above is only ever blue.

'Look, Danny,' Abi says as she takes his hand and leads him to the balcony. 'The stars.'

ACKNOWLEDGEMENTS

I would like to think my fellow writers in Thursday Night Writers, Tralee, for all their feedback and support over the past few years, especially Martin O'Brien, Ashling Dennehy, Ania Dokurno, Eadbhard McGowan, Davena O'Neill, Gordon Pinckheard, and Chris Zerillo.

A very special thank you to Ed Valfre, photographer extraordinaire for the stunning cover shot.

And to Dave Borrowdale and Reflex Press for making this collection possible. An amazing editor and press! Thank you so much for publishing my debut collection and making my dream come true.

Thanks also to the editors who previously published some of these pieces in their literary zines. Without your support, this collection would never have come to be.

Finally, I'd like to thank my sons, Ronan and Liam, for their patience and love. Everything is all for you. Always.

*

The author and publisher wish to thank the editors of the journals in which the following stories were first published:

'Some Days Are Better Than Ours' was first published in *Spelk*, January 2019; 'Various Things That Crossed Her Mind', *Ghost Parachute*, March 2019; 'Porcelain', *The Fiction Pool*, February 2017; 'I Eat the Flowers on Your Grave', *Anti-Heroin Chic*, February 2019; 'All the Things We Cannot Say', *Ellipsis Zine*, March 2019 'I Walked 10,000 Worlds for You', *NewMag*, February 2019; 'Bear', *Fictive Dream*, February 2019; 'Opium', *The Cabinet of Heed*, October 2017; 'Resurrection', *Virtual Zine*, March 2019; 'Old Woman in a Black Buick Tripping on Nine Inch Nails', *Litro*, May 2019; 'Yellow', *The Cabinet of Heed*, April 2018.